Follow me!

Story written by Gill Munton
Illustrated by Tim Archbold

Speed Sounds

Consonants   *Ask children to say the sounds.*

f	l	m	n	r	s	v	z	sh	th	ng
ff	ll	mm	**nn**	rr	ss	ve	**zz**			nk
	le		**kn**		se		se			
					ce		s			

b	c	d	g	h	j	p	qu	t	w	x	y	**ch**
bb	k	dd	gg			pp		tt	wh			tch
	ck											

Each box contains one sound but sometimes more than one grapheme.
*Focus graphemes for this story are **circled**.*

Vowels

Ask children to say the sounds in and out of order.

a	e ea	i	o	u	ay	ee y	igh	**ow**
at	hen	in	on	up	day	see	high	blow

oo	oo	ar	or oor ore	air	ir	ou	oy
zoo	look	car	for	fair	whirl	shout	boy

Story Green Words

Ask children to read the words first in Fred Talk and then say the word.

Dizzy Duck   Crow   cheep   pond   row
bank   splash   twig   tow

Ask children to say the syllables and then read the whole word.

duck|ling   will|ow   can|not

Ask children to read the root first and then the whole word with the suffix.

follow → followed   stay → stayed

cheep → cheeped

Red Words

said	he	me	you
to	do	what	no
the	your	her	she
all	I've	are	go

Follow me!

Dizzy Duck had three yellow ducklings.

Cheep!   Cheep!   Cheep!

"Let's go and swim
in the pond,"
said Dizzy. "Follow me!"

The ducklings sat in a row on the bank.

"Do you know what to do?"

said Dizzy.

"No," said the ducklings.

"Then I will show you," said Dizzy.

"Follow me."

Splash!

Duckling 1 followed.

Splash!

Duckling 2 followed.

Splash!

But Duckling 3 stayed on the bank.

"I cannot swim!" he cheeped.

"I will help you," said Crow.

"I will get a twig from that

willow tree, and throw it

into the pond.

Jump on the twig —

and I will tow you along!"

Questions to talk about

Ask children to TTYP for each question using 'Fastest finger' (FF) or 'Have a think' (HaT).

p.8 (FF)   Why is Dizzy taking the ducklings to the pond?

p.9 (HaT)   What does Dizzy Duck want to teach the ducklings?

p.10 (FF)   What does Dizzy tell them to do?

p.11 (HaT)   Why does Duckling 3 stay on the bank?

p.12 (FF)   How does Crow say he will help the duckling?

p.13 (FF)   What does Crow do when Duckling 3 is on the twig?